W9-BVG-046

BOOK THREE

GOOD CROOKS

Sniff a Skunk!

BOOK THREE

GOOD CROOKS

Sniff a Skunk!

Mary Amato

Illustrated by **Ward Jenkins**

EGMONT
Publishing
NEW YORK

EGMONT

We bring stories to life

First published by Egmont Publishing, 2015
443 Park Avenue South, Suite 806
New York, NY 10016

Text copyright © Mary Amato, 2015
Illustrations copyright © Ward Jenkins, 2015
All rights reserved

1 3 5 7 9 8 6 4 2

www.egmontusa.com
www.maryamato.com
www.wardjenkins.com.com

Library of Congress Cataloging-in-Publication Data
Amato, Mary.
Sniff a skunk! / Mary Amato ; illustrated by Ward Jenkins.
pages cm. -- (Good Crooks ; book 3)
Summary: Unlike their thieving parents, ten-year-old twins
Billy and Jillian Crook like to do good deeds, including
rescuing a baby skunk. Features activities.
ISBN 978-1-60684-598-1 (hardcover)
[1. Conduct of life--Fiction. 2. Robbers and outlaws--Fiction.
3. Brothers and sisters--Fiction. 4. Twins--Fiction.
5. Skunks--Fiction.] I. Jenkins, Ward, illustrator. II. Title.
PZ7.A49165So 2015
[Fic]--dc23   2014040414

ISBN 978-1-60684-600-1 (eBook)
ISBN 978-1-60684-599-8 (paperback)

Printed in the United States of America

Contents

Every Bootie Needs a Boost

Tap! Tap! Tap!

I was asleep when I felt a tap on my head.

Then I smelled it. A horrible, stinky smell. Was a pig trying to kiss me? Did a fish fly through the window and die on my pillow? Did I forget to floss again?

"Billy!"

I opened my eyes.

My twin sister Jillian's face was close to mine. Her stinky morning breath was coming at me.

She leaned closer. "What do you want to do today?"

"I'm still sleeping." I pushed her away. "Please go say hello to your toothbrush."

She pulled me out of bed. I landed on the floor with a thump.

"What do you really, really, really want to do today?" she asked. She was serious.

There was no use going back to sleep. I got up and looked out the window. Sunlight was streaming through the trees. Birds were chirping. The day was opening its eyes and smiling like a big cute baby.

What did I really want to do today? The answer bubbled up from the bottom of my soul. I knew what I wanted to do. It was a mad, crazy thing.

"Go ahead, Billy," Jillian whispered. "Say it."

I spread my arms wide and said: "I want to do a good deed!"

"Shh!" she whispered. "Don't say it so loud! What if Mom and Dad hear you?"

Our parents are Ron and Tanya

Crook. Yep, the famous robbers. They want us to steal, lie, and cheat like them.

"Mom wants us to find them a new store to rob," I said.

"I know," Jillian said. "I don't want to be a crook. I want to do good deeds, too."

"We're not like Mom and Dad at all," I said.

Jillian nodded. "Do you think they're our real parents?"

"They steal a lot of stuff," I said. "Maybe they stole us."

"Maybe they stole us from our real parents at the hospital when we were just born," Jillian said.

I looked at myself in the mirror. "I was such a cute baby, everybody probably wanted to steal me."

Jillian laughed. "Let's go to the hospital and search for clues. Mom and Dad said we were born there. Maybe we can find out if we were stolen."

I gave her a thumbs-up.

"Hey, I got us new disguises," she said.

Crooks always have to wear disguises when we leave the house. We have lots of costumes, wigs, masks, and even fake rear ends. Why fake rear ends? So nobody recognizes us from behind!

"*Tada!*" Jillian said, and showed me our new outfits.

PeeWee Patrol Club uniforms!

We put them on.

"I always wanted to be in the PeeWee Patrol Club!" I said. "PeeWees do good deeds, like help kids cross the street safely and visit sick people."

"I know! Come on. We need to get to the hospital and back before Mom and Dad wake up."

"Wait!" I grabbed one of my fake rear ends. It was called the Bootie Booster. I stuffed the Bootie Booster down the back of my pants. "Now I'm ready for action."

Jillian giggled.

We tiptoed into the hallway.

Urrr. The floor creaked.

"Ssh! Be quiet," Jillian whispered.

Tip . . . tip . . . tip. We tiptoed past our parents' bedroom door.

Snore . . . snore . . . snore. Dad was snoring away.

Tip . . . tip . . . urrr! Another creaky step.

Uh-oh! The snoring stopped. We froze.

A few seconds later: *Snore . . . snore . . . snore.*

Whew.

Jillian gave me a thumbs-up. Carefully we tiptoed down the stairs. We were going to make it!

By the door, there was a mirror. I stopped to look at myself. My PeeWee Patrol uniform was awesome. And what a cutie bootie!

I started dancing. I know all the moves.

"Come on, Billy," Jillian whispered.

"I'm doing it PeeWee style." I hopped around in a circle, shaking my bootie. "Check out how good I loo—"

My arm
knocked against
a vase. The vase
went flying—
it was going
to crash into a
million pieces.

I dove for it. "Whoa!" I caught it in midair! Then I fell right on my bootie.

Thump!

Our parents came flying down the stairs.

I put the vase back.

"What are you two doing up so early?" Mom asked.

"And why are you dressed like that?" Dad added.

I looked at Jillian. Jillian looked at me.

"We . . . we . . . ," Jillian stammered.

"I know what you're doing," Mom said.

"You do?" I gulped.

"You're going to find us a new store to rob!" She smiled at Dad. "We have great kids, don't we, Ron?"

"We do!" Dad gave us each a pat on the back. "Okay, kids, have fun! We're going back to sleep."

Our parents went back up the stairs. Jillian and I slipped out the door.

"That was close," Jillian said. "Come on!"

I stopped.

"What are you doing now?" she asked.

"I'm having a moment of thanks."

"For what?"

"For the Bootie Booster." I patted my fake rear end. "Thanks for the safe landing, Bootie. You're the best."

Yikes! Stripes!

We walked on our secret mission to the hospital. It was early. The street was quiet. Then . . .

Plunk. Plunk. Plunk.

Jillian and I stopped.

"Shh," Jillian whispered. "Did you hear something?"

Plunk. Plunk. Plunk.

I heard something. I just didn't know what it was.

"Footsteps?" I wondered.

"I don't know," she whispered. "I hope Mom and Dad aren't following us."

"Me, too," I whispered back.

We both turned around to look. The sidewalk was empty, but somebody could have been hiding behind a tree.

We had to be very careful. We kept walking.

Plunk. Plunk. Plunk.

It didn't sound like footsteps. It sounded like something was dropping onto the ground.

After a moment, we heard something else: "Oooch. Oooch. Oooch." A sad sound.

"Is that a dog crying?" my sister whispered.

"We have to check it out," I said.

We followed the noise and peeked around a big tree. On a patch of grass, a small animal was crouched. She was a little ball of black fur. Both of her paws were covering her eyes.

Nuts lay on the ground all around her. Acorns.

Plunk!

An acorn hit the little animal on her head.

"Oooch!" she whimpered.

"Check out the stripe on her back! She's a skunk!" Jillian said.

We stepped back.

The skunk whimpered and covered her head with her paws.

Plunk! Another acorn flew down and hit her back.

"Oooch." The skunk's legs were shaking.

We looked up. A squirrel was sitting on a branch in a tree.

"Hee-hee-hee." The squirrel laughed. He had a pile of nuts in his hands, ready to throw.

Jillian took another step back.

"Skunks use their stinky spray to defend themselves," Jillian said. "That skunk is going to spray."

"Maybe she doesn't know how," I said. "She looks like a baby."

"Hee-hee-hee." The squirrel threw another nut.

"Stop that," I said to the squirrel.

"Hee-hee-hee," he laughed.

"Come on," Jillian said. "I'm sure that skunk is going to spray. If we smell like skunk, they won't let us in the hospital."

We kept walking. Then I heard a sound.

PLUNK!

Tip, tip, tip . . .

I turned around. The skunk was following us. She looked at me with her big black eyes.

"Stinkball wants us to protect her," I said.

"Stinkball?" Jillian turned around. "Oh, hi, Stinkball. You can't come with us. They won't let us come into the hospital with you." She pointed her finger at Stinkball. "Stay!"

Stinkball looked at me.

"You've got to find your family, Stinkball," I said. "I'm very cute, but I ain't your daddy."

We walked a few steps.

"Hee-hee-hee."

The squirrel threw another nut.

I got mad. "We can't let that squirrel bully poor Stinkball," I said.

"You're right," Jillian said. "We need to help." She looked up at the squirrel. "I am using a firm but friendly voice. Go away."

The squirrel threw another nut.

"Ooch, ooch." Poor Stinkball was scared.

"The problem is the squirrel isn't scared of us," Jillian said. "He sees humans all the time. He's used to us."

That gave me an idea. I crouched down and took a deep breath.

"What are you doing?" Jillian asked.

"Shh! I'm getting into character."

I started pounding the ground with my fists. My face turned red.

Jillian and Stinkball backed away.

I growled. Then I jumped up and roared. I bellowed. I flexed my muscles and hopped from foot to foot like a mad, crazy baboon.

The squirrel's jaw dropped. He let go of all the nuts he was holding. *Zoom!* He was off, hopping from branch to branch until he was out of sight.

Stinkball peered out from behind a tree.

"That nut-chunking punk is gone now," I said. "It's okay."

Stinkball wiggled her rear end happily.

"I'm glad you found a way to scare that squirrel," Jillian said. "I don't think he's coming back! You did a good deed for Stinkball."

A warm, wonderful feeling filled me from the tip of my toes to the tip of my nose. "It feels good to do good," I said to my sister.

Jillian nodded. "I know! We can't be Crooks. Come on, let's find out if we were stolen from the hospital."

I pointed to a bush. "See, Stinkball? You can hide in there."

Stinkball scampered under the bush.

"Come on, Billy."

"Bye, Stinkball!" I waved.

In the shadows of the bush, I could see a tiny smile.

Knock, Knock!

We walked into the hospital. Mmmmn . . . a delicious smell drifted into my nostrils. It was coming from the gift shop. Chocolate . . . bubble gum . . .

"Let's stop and get some candy," I said. I pulled Jillian in. The store was filled with teddy bears, flowers, balloons, cookies, and candy.

"They're only missing one thing," I said.

"Let me guess," she said. "Bacon?"

I fist-bumped her. Anybody who knows me, Billy Crook, knows I loves me my bacon.

She tried to pull me out of the shop. "We don't have time! Come on."

I pulled one way. She pulled the other. She won. That girl could win a tug-of-war with a crocodile.

She marched us to the hospital's information desk.

"Hello, PeeWees," the woman at the desk said. "We love how the PeeWees come on Saturdays to help out."

"Hello," Jillian said. "We're doing a project on hospital safety. We were wondering if any babies were ever stolen from this hospital."

"Oh, dear!" the woman said. "I hope not, but I don't know. Ask one of the nurses who works in the nursery. That's on the third floor."

"Thank you," we both said. We walked back toward the elevator. We were excited.

A man holding balloons and a teddy bear ran out of the gift shop. "There you are, PeeWees! Thank goodness you're here! I'm Mr. Packard. I work here in the gift shop. Please take these to room 215." He handed

me the bear and Jillian the balloons.
"When you're done, come down to the
shop. We have a lot of gifts to deliver
today."

"Let's do this good deed first,"
Jillian whispered to me. "Then we'll
go up to the nursery and search for
clues."

I nodded. "Wait, Mr. Packard. I
have a question."

"Yes?"

"You've got teddy bears. Why not teddy skunks?"

Mr. Packard laughed. He thought I was joking!

We found room 215 on the second floor and walked in. An old man was lying in bed looking out the window. He was alone and looked sick and sad.

"We need to help him get his cheer on," Jillian whispered to me.

"No problemo," I told Jillian. Then I called out to the man, "Happy birthday!"

He turned to look at us. "It's not my birthday," he said.

"Well, it should be!" I marched over to his bed with the bear. Jillian came with the balloons. A little card

26

was taped to the balloons. It said:

Get well, Mr. Henry.
From Jenny and Frank.

We could do better than that.

"These come with a free song!" I said.

"They do?" Mr. Henry asked.

"They do?" Jillian asked.

"Yep. Jillian, get a beat going for me with your feet." I turned to Mr. Henry. "My sister makes loud beats because she has very big feets."

He smiled.

Jillian started stomping a beat.

It was working already.

I started stomping, too. I was getting my groove on.

"Stuck in a room? Feeling down?
All you got to wear is a hospital
    gown?
Let us in now. We'll be your
    medicine now.
We'll turn that frown right upside
    down.
You're gonna get well, we can tell,
    let's yell!
Shake it up, shake it down. Shake
    it, baby, to this sound.
Shake it up, shake it down. Shake
    your feet right off the ground.
Shake it up, shake it down. Shake
    it all around the town."

Mr. Henry sat up and clapped.

"Happy birthday, even though it's not your birthday," Jillian added.

"That just made my day!" he said.
"Do it again." He got out of bed and
took the balloons from us and danced
around as we sang the song.

The nurse walked in with a lunch
tray.

"Food!" Mr. Henry said. "Bring it
on!"

"Wow! Mr. Henry hasn't eaten in two days," the nurse said. "This is great."

"It's my birthday. It's my birthday." Mr. Henry pumped his hands in the air.

"It is?" the nurse asked.

"No, but it should be!" Mr. Henry said, and took the sandwich off the tray.

We promised to visit again and walked out.

"Doing good deeds is like eating a great bacon burger," I said.

"What do you mean?" Jillian asked.

"You want to keep doing more."

"I know! Let's deliver one more

gift," Jillian said. "Then we'll go to the nursery."

"Sounds like a plan. Wait." I stopped and looked at Jillian's feet.

"What are you doing?" she asked.

"I'm having a moment of thanks."

"For what?"

I smiled. "I can always count on your great big feet for giving me a great big beat. Thanks!"

She laughed.

Goo, Goo, Goop!

We raced back down to the gift shop. Mr. Packard gave us a basket of cookies to deliver.

"Take these to room 311," he said. "Third floor."

Jillian took the cookies and smiled at me. "The third floor!" she whispered. "That's where we want to go!"

Kids, toddlers, and babies were on the third floor. My nose told me that some stinky diapers were hanging out there, too. "If only Stinkball could smell this, maybe she'd learn how to make stinkers of her own," I said to Jillian.

We found room 311 and walked in.

A kid was in the bed. She was about five years old. Her mom was sitting next to her.

"We have cookies for you," Jillian said. "Sorry you're in the hospital."

The girl didn't smile.

"She misses her friends and her school," her mom said. "I can't cheer her up."

"This calls for some funny faces," I said.

The kid looked at me.

"Definitely not my mad, crazy baboon face," I said. "Because that would scare the pants off you if you were wearing pants."

The girl smiled.

"Maybe . . . my teenage mutant naked mole-rat faces! I have a whole bunch of those."

The girl's smile got bigger.

"You ready?"

She nodded. I stuck my front teeth out and let the funny faces roll.

The girl and her mom both laughed.

Jillian handed them the cookies.

"Thanks, guys," the mom said. "You really helped."

We said good-bye and danced out the door.

A nurse walked by with a baby in her arms.

"Look!" Jillian said. We ran to catch up with her.

"Excuse me," Jillian said. "Is the nursery here?"

"Yes." The nurse smiled. "You can come and look in the window. I'm going there now."

We followed her.

"Do you know if babies have ever been stolen from this hospital?" I asked.

"My goodness!" The nurse gasped. "That would be terrible. I don't know. I just started working here."

"How could we find out?" Jillian asked. "We're learning about hospital safety."

"There's an office on the first floor where they keep records of all the babies born here. You could go there." The nurse stopped. "Here's the nursery."

There was a room with a big window. The nurse took the baby inside. Through the window we saw a whole bunch of babies in little cribs! Some were bald. Some had hair. They were all cute. One little guy with fuzzy curls was crying.

"Come on," Jillian said. "Let's go down to that office."

"Okay, but first let me cheer up that little guy."

I made my naked mole-rat faces. The baby stopped crying.

"It worked," I said. "I'm awesome."

"Newborns can't even see," Jillian said. "He stopped crying because that nurse just picked him up."

The nurse brought him over to the window so we could see him.

I waved. "Babies and skunks love me," I said to Jillian. "I have made several new tiny friends today."

My new tiny friend opened his mouth.

"Aw. See, Jillian? He's going to smile at me. Goo, goo!"

Just then a big white stream of vomit gushed out of my new friend's tiny mouth. The goop landed with a splash on the glass right in front of my face.

I've never been so grateful for a window in my life.

Bad Doctors

"Come on," Jillian said. "Let's go to that office on the first floor and find out if we were stolen from here ten years ago."

I waved good-bye to the babies. "I'll come back and visit you!" I said. "But I ain't changing any stinking diapers!"

Jillian laughed and pulled me along.

Just as we got off the elevator on

the main floor, two doctors walked out of a supply closet. They saw us and walked toward us.

"Oh, no," Jillian said. She turned so the doctors couldn't see her and made a face.

"Are you having a heart attack?" I asked. "Should I get one of the doctors to help?"

"Those doctors aren't doctors," she whispered. "They're our so-called parents. Ron and Tanya Crook! They must have tracked us here and changed into those disguises."

"Rats! I feel sick to my stomach," I said.

Jillian sighed. "Well, at least you're in a hospital, bro."

"Hey, kids," Dad whispered. "What are you doing here?"

"We thought you were finding us a place to rob," Mom said. "Don't tell me you're doing something nice! Are you visiting sick people?"

"We—we—" Jillian couldn't think of what to say.

I changed the subject. "I bet you guys want to buy your kids a present!"

I gave them my killer smile and stepped back into the gift shop. "Just look at these cute teddy bears."

The place was packed. Lots of people were buying gifts.

Mom's eyebrows went up. "Oh, I know why you're here."

Jillian and I looked at each other.

"You *did* find a new place to rob!" Mom said.

"The hospital gift shop," Dad said. "What a great idea. That cash register will be full by the end of the day!"

"We'll come back tonight and steal it all." Mom gave us each a pat on the back. "You guys can go home now."

Mr. Packard walked over.

In a loud, fake voice, Dad said to us, "We love the PeeWee Patrol.

Thanks for coming in to help." He turned to Mr. Packard. "These little PeeWees have to run home. We know their mommy and daddy, and they want them home for lunch."

"Okay, thanks." Mr. Packard waved. "Come back again, PeeWees!"

Mom and Dad walked us to the front door. "We'll meet you at home later. We want to scope out where the security guards stand."

Sadly, Jillian and I walked out the door and headed for home.

"I feel terrible," she whispered.

"Me, too," I whispered back.

"We didn't find out if we were stolen from here as babies," she said. "And now, because of us, the gift shop is going to get robbed."

"I don't want that gift shop to get robbed. All the people in the hospital are so nice."

"I know," Jillian said.

As we turned the corner, we both heard a sound behind us.

Tip, tip, tip . . .

Someone was following us!

We stopped walking, and the noise stopped. We started walking, and the noise started again. *Tip, tip, tip* . . .

Jillian whispered, "I hope Mom and Dad aren't spying on us."

"Let's look," I whispered. "On the count of three. One, two, three!"

We both turned.

My tiny friend Stinkball was following us again. She froze, putting her paws over her eyes.

"Hi, Stinkball," Jillian said.

The skunk lowered her paws and blinked at us.

"She looks sad," Jillian said.

Above us, the leaves in the tree rustled. The skunk looked up and started to shake.

"She looks scared, too," I added.

"I wonder why she doesn't defend herself," Jillian said.

"Maybe she got separated from her mom and dad before they could teach her," I replied.

"I think you're right. Now Stinkball is following us because she is scared of that squirrel," Jillian said. "She wants us to protect her."

"You can protect yourself, dude," I told the skunk. "You have an awesome superpower. The superpower of stink! Use it or lose it!"

Stinkball just looked up at us with her big black eyes.

"I think she needs our help," Jillian said. "Let's teach her how to be a skunk. Then we can go home and figure out how to stop Mom and Dad from robbing that gift shop."

"It's a plan." I turned to the skunk. "Stinkball, we are going to teach you how to get stinky. If I can do it, you can do it!"

The Skunk and the Punk

"If we are going to help Stinkball, we need to learn more about skunks." Jillian took out her smartphone. "Let's do some research."

We found a park and sat down on a bench. Stinkball followed us and hid behind a garbage can. She kept peeking out, though. Stinky School was starting, and our student was listening.

Jillian typed in the word *skunk* and found a page of skunk facts. "Okay, Stinkball, you eat at night and sleep during the day. So you should be sleeping right now."

Stinkball looked clueless.

"It's daytime, dude! You shouldn't even be out. You should be sleeping. You know, snoozing, snoring, catching some z's." I hit the ground and started snoring.

Stinkball tried it.

"Good job!" Jillian said. "Okay, sleep during the day and eat at night. Got it?"

Stinkball nodded. I jumped up. "Hey, what do skunks eat?"

"Bugs, worms, fruit, plants . . ."

I shook my head. "Dude, you don't know what you're missing. You got to chomp on a bacon cheeseburger."

Stinkball made a face.

"Okay. Okay. Bugs it is." I crouched down and looked in the grass. A black beetle was crawling around. "See? Your food isn't going to jump into your mouth, dude. You got to hunt for it. Look down. What do you see?"

Stinkball looked down.

"See a bug? Just stick your face down in there and gobble it up."

Stinkball looked at me.

"Don't make me show you, dude."

Jillian laughed. "Show her. I dare you."

The beetle had dotted wings and hairy legs. I gazed down at it and thought: Sometimes a guy has to do what a skunk has to do. I took a deep breath, stuck my face down, and gobbled up that beetle.

Jillian almost lost it. "Gross!"

"Crunchy, but a little dry," I said. "Could use some ketchup."

She laughed.

Another bug popped up in the grass near the skunk.

"Now, come on, Stinkball," I said. "If I can do it, you can do it!"

Stinkball pounced. And missed.

"I think you'll have to do a lot of practicing with Stinkball," Jillian said.

"Dude," I said to Stinkball, "you are going to owe me big time."

Jillian went back to her research. "Okay. Here's another fact. 'Babies are born in late spring and stay with their moms until the fall.'"

"Dude, where's your mom?" I asked.

"Oom, oom." The skunk blinked.

"Aw, that's one sad sound," I said.

"Skunks sometimes carry rabies, so you should never try to pet one," Jillian said.

"Besides that, they stink!" I said.

"Not really. It says here that they are very clean. They only spray to defend themselves," Jillian said. "They can't run fast, so they defend themselves with their aroma."

"Hear that, Stinkball?" I said. "Every time you see a squirrel, just let it rip."

"No," Jillian said. "That's not how it works. They don't walk around spraying all the time. It's a last resort. They have a whole routine for defending themselves."

"Hear that, Stinkball?" I said. "You have a whole routine. I can't keep chasing away squirrels for you. You can defend yourself, okay?"

Stinkball grabbed her tail. She looked like she wasn't sure.

"First you stomp your front feet," Jillian said. "Then you raise your tail and arch your back and hiss."

"Cool. It's like saying, Get out of my face, dude!" I stomped my feet, stuck my rear end out like I was raising my tail, then arched my back and hissed. "Now you try. Look tough when you do it."

Stinkball tried. She looked cute instead of tough.

"Okay," I said. "We'll keep working on that."

"Here's another fact," Jillian said. "Sometimes skunks do handstands to scare off other animals."

"Handstands?" I laughed. "That's like a ninja move!" I did a handstand and then popped back onto my feet. "Ai ya!" I did a karate chop in the air.

Stinkball jumped onto her hands and fell over.

"That's okay—you'll get it," I said.

"And if all of those things don't work and the skunk is still threatened," Jillian explained, "then it turns and sprays. You can spray up to ten feet, Stinkball."

"That is awesome!" I said. "I wish I could do that."

Jillian rolled her eyes. "You make bad enough stinks."

I turned around and stuck my rear end out again. "Just lift your tail and spray!"

Stinkball turned around and wiggled her rear end.

Nothing. Nada. Zip.

Jillian's phone buzzed.

"It's a text from Mom and Dad," she said. "They're home. They're wondering why we're not."

"Stinkball, we have to get home. But this lesson ain't over," I said.

"Follow us and we'll keep working on your ninja skunk moves."

"We have to keep this a secret, though," Jillian said to Stinkball. "Our parents, Ron and Tanya Crook, would not like us doing a good deed for a skunk!"

"If Stinkball does make a stink, we won't be able to keep that a secret," I said.

Jillian patted me on the back. "That's okay. They'll just think it was you."

7

Stinky Style

Home sweet home.

"Stinkball, wait in the backyard."
I pointed. "We'll be right out."

Our parents had changed into
their regular clothes and were eating
lunch.

"Hey, guys, what took you so
long?" Mom asked.

"Jillian has big feet," I said, "but
they're slow feet."

Dad laughed.

"Thanks for the great idea to rob the gift shop," Mom said.

"Yeah. When we're done with lunch, we're going to take a nap so we'll be ready for tonight!" Dad said.

"Why don't you guys practice that lesson on picking pockets we taught you?" Mom asked.

"Okay," Jillian said. "Let's do it in the backyard, Billy." She gave me a secret look.

"The backyard!" I said. "Great idea."

We changed into our Crook clothes, and Jillian got supplies ready. As soon as we heard our parents go into their bedroom, we went outside.

"Time for your lesson, Stinkball," I said.

"Okay, we're going to start with some warm-ups," I said. "Jog in place. Hup, two, three, four." Jillian and I jogged in place. Stinkball looked at us like we were crazy.

"Come on, dude," I said. "Hup, two, three, four."

Stinkball started jogging.

"All right. Now, when a bully comes, the first thing you do is stomp," I said. "Let's practice. We're going to stomp twelve times! Hup, two, three, four."

We stomped twelve times. Stinkball stomped, too.

"All right! Pump those arms when you stomp. Look tough. Let's do it again!" I cheered.

We stomped.

"Now we're going to make a hiss and put up our claws. Ninja style. Twelve times. Hup, two, three, four."

We hissed and clawed. Stinkball was getting it.

"Let's flex our arm muscles next." I made a muscle.

"I don't think skunks really do that," Jillian said.

"But it looks cool," I replied.

We flexed our arm muscles. We looked cool.

Stinkball was feeling more powerful. I could tell.

"Okay, Stinkball. Now we're going to put it all together," I said.

"Jillian, give me a beat with your great big feet," I said. "A big whompy beat."

Jillian stomped her feet.

Whomp. Whomp. Whomp.
Whomp. Whomp. Whomp.

I got the beat going in my feet.

"You're so cool. You're so black.
Got a white stripe down your
back.

*Whomp. Whomp. Whomp. Do it
   Stinky style."*

Stinkball looked at me like I was crazy. "Come on, Stinkball. You're powerful. You just got to *feel* powerful. Start by pumping your legs up and down and showing off that white stripe. Pump. Pump. Pump. Come on, Jillian. You do it, too, so Stinkball gets the idea."

*"You're so cool. You're so black.
Got a white stripe down your back.
Whomp. Whomp. Whomp. Do it
   Stinky style."*

Stinkball started to get her groove going.

"Okay now," I said. "Here comes the next part.

"Stomp your feet. Raise your tail.
You got moves. You will not fail.
Whomp. Whomp. Whomp. Do it
Stinky style."

Jillian and I stomped our feet twice, popped our booties up, and flexed our arms.

"Come on, do it with us!"

We got the beat going again.

"Stomp your feet. Raise your
tail.
You got moves. You will not fail.
Whomp. Whomp. Whomp. Do it
Stinky style."

Stinkball stomped her feet, raised her tail, and flexed her arms.

"Oh, yeah. You got it!" Jillian said. "Okay, here we go."

"Make a hiss. Stomp your feet.
Arch your back. Jump to the beat.
Whomp. Whomp. Whomp. Do it
Stinky style."

To the beat, Stinkball made a hiss, stomped her feet, arched her back, and jumped!

"Go, Stinkball!" Jillian said.

"Okay, we're saving the best for last," I said.

"Don't be scared. Don't be blinky. Turn around and make a stinky!"

I turned around, stuck out my bootie like I was lifting my tail, and made a *pssssst!* sound.

Stinkball turned around and lifted her tail.

A horrible smell filled the air.

Jillian plugged her nose and jumped up and down. "It worked! It worked!"

"Actually," I said, "that was me."

Jillian sighed. "Stinkball learned everything but the most important part."

"Turn around and make a stinky," I said to the skunk.

Stinkball turned around and lifted her tail, but nothing came out.

"She doesn't get it," I said.

"Turn and *spray*," Jillian said.

Stinkball looked clueless.

"Let it rip," I said.

Stinkball lifted her tail. Finally

. . . *Psst* . . . A smell came out. It wasn't much, but it was a little stinky.

"That's it!" I jumped up and down.

"You got it," Jillian said.

"You made a little stinky. You made a little stinky!" I sang, and danced around.

Stinkball grinned from ear to ear.

8

Ready . . . Aim . . . *Psssssst!*

"**H**ee-hee-hee."

We looked up.

That mean squirrel was back! He was perched on a tree limb, holding a handful of nuts.

"Here's your chance," Jillian said to our skunk friend.

Stinkball looked at us. She was scared.

"You can do it," I whispered.

Jillian nodded. "You have to try!"

We hid behind a tree.

"We'll be right here," I whispered. "We'll talk you through it. Don't worry."

The squirrel looked at Stinkball with a gleam in his eyes and let one fly.

Plunk!

Stinkball ducked, and the nut missed.

"Come on, Stinkball," I said. "You have to stand up and be a skunk. Remember: 'Stomp your feet. Raise your tail. You got moves. You will not fail.'"

Stinkball looked at me. Then she looked at the squirrel.

"Hee-hee-hee," said the squirrel. He picked up another nut and was about to throw it.

Whomp. Whomp. Whomp.

Stinkball stomped her feet.

Whomp. Whomp. Whomp.

"Look!" Jillian said. "She's starting to defend herself."

Stinkball raised her tail.

The squirrel just laughed.

Another nut came flying. *Zoom . . . plunk!*

It hit poor Stinkball right on her bootie. Stinkball looked at us again.

"'Don't be scared. Don't be blinky. Turn around and make a stinky,'" I whispered.

Stinkball turned around and lifted her tail. Nothing happened.

"Hee-hee-hee." The squirrel wound up for the pitch.

"Let it rip, Stinkball!" I cheered.

Stinkball lifted her tail higher and . . . *pssst* . . . It wasn't a huge stink, but it was bigger than the last one. The spray hit that squirrel in the face. He dropped the nuts and ran.

"Go, Stinkball!" We cheered.

We were all jumping and cheering. Then Jillian stopped. She had an idea. I could tell by the gleam in her eyes.

"We could use Stinkball to help us stop the robbery," she said. "We could get Stinkball to hide by our front door. When Mom and Dad come out to go to the hospital, Stinkball can spray them."

"Great idea," I said. "But

it's got to be a
big, bad smell.
Then they won't
be able to go
anywhere. If they
tried to rob a place,

the police would be able to follow their
scent."

I turned to Stinkball. "We have a
job for you. It might be dangerous. Are
you in?"

Stinkball flexed her muscles.

We laughed.

She jumped up and down. She was
excited to help us.

"All this is making me hungry.
Let's celebrate with lunch," I said.

We made sandwiches and brought
them outside to eat.

"Stinkball, eat up!" I said. "We have a big job tonight. You need your strength."

Stinkball looked at me.

"I think she needs one more bug-eating lesson," Jillian said.

"Great." I rolled my eyes.

After watching me catch a bunch of bugs, Stinkball finally got the idea.

A juicy bug appeared. Stinkball caught it and chomped down on that bug. She smiled.

I helped her! That warm, wonderful feeling filled me again.

"You did a good job teaching her," Jillian said. "It must feel good."

"It will feel even better now that I can stop eating bugs," I said. *"Blech!"*

Sneaking Out

After lunch, we told Stinkball to take a nap.

We went inside. Our parents were still napping.

I yawned. "I think I'll take a snooze, too."

Jillian poked me. "No. We have too much to do. I am going to invent special goggles and headsets for us. Stinkball's goggles will have a built-in video camera, and ours will have built-in miniscreens. That way we can see whatever she sees. I'll add headphones with walkie-talkie microphones so we can tell Stinkball what to do. After we put her by the front door, we can go back up to our rooms. We can give her the command to spray from there. Ron and Tanya will never guess we did it."

"Cool! What should I do?"

"Spy on Mom and Dad. If they wake up, keep them busy until I'm done."

Here's what Jillian did:

Here's what I did:

Jillian poked me again. "It's late," she whispered. "You fell asleep. You should have been spying."

Suddenly, we heard our parents talking. We put our ears against their bedroom door.

"Let's bring the kids. We can show them how it's done."

"No," Mom said. "They've been acting strange lately. They might mess it up. Let's wait till they're asleep and then go out."

The door opened, and we both tumbled in.

"Hello, Mumsy and Popsy," I said. "We were just coming in to ask what's for dinner."

"We're hungry," Jillian said.

"Yeah, and I'm tired of eating bugs."

Dad laughed. He thought I was joking.

After dinner, we told our parents we wanted to go to bed early. We put pillows in our beds and wigs on our pillows to make it look like we were sleeping. Then we tiptoed down the hall. We had to put the headset on Stinkball, show her where to wait, and then get back up to our room without being caught.

Our parents were downstairs

in the living room watching their favorite TV show: *The World's Greatest Criminals.*

"Wait!" I whispered. "I forgot my Bootie Booster."

"We don't have time!" Jillian pulled me down the stairs.

Tip . . . tip . . . urrr.

We froze.

"Hard to be sneaky when floors are creaky," I whispered.

"Shh!" she whispered.

We made it out the door. We ran around to the backyard.

"Stinkball?" I whispered.

No Stinkball.

What if the squirrel had come and chased Stinkball away? What if a mean dog had come and decided to use Stinkball as a chew toy?

The bush next to the house rustled. A small black shape crawled out.

Stinkball!

Jillian helped us into all our gear. We looked awesome.

I pulled out a picture of our parents. "These are our parents, Ron and Tanya Crook," I told Stinkball. "When you see them, spray them!"

She turned around and lifted her tail.

"No! Don't spray the picture. Wait until we give you the cue. Don't spray until we say so. Okay?"

Stinkball nodded.

"Positions!" Jillian said.

I showed Stinkball where to wait by the door.

"We're going back inside, Stinkball," Jillian said. "Wait for our cue."

We were about to open the door when we heard our parents' voices. Ron and Tanya were coming out. Oh, no! They must have seen that we were sleeping and decided to leave early.

We ducked into the shadow behind the door and peeked.

They stepped out, dressed in their doctor disguises again. If we told Stinkball to spray, our parents would hear us. We didn't move.

Stinkball froze, too.

Our parents hopped in the car and pulled out.

They were going to rob the gift shop. We had missed our chance!

10

Faster than a
Speeding Wheelchair

"Now what?" I asked Jillian.

"We have to get there fast," she said.

"But they're driving. They'll be done with the job before we can even make it there."

Jillian laughed. "Billy, Billy, Billy. You should know me better than that." She ran to the garage and pulled

out another invention: a wheelchair
outfitted with jetpacks. "Nobody will
notice if we have a wheelchair outside
the hospital. Hop on, Billy boy! We'll
get them before they go into the
hospital."

"Woohoo!" I yelled. "But wait!
What about Stinkball? Skunks can't
run fast, remember?"

She grabbed my skateboard
and attached it to the back of the
wheelchair with a rope. "Hop on,
Stinkball."

Jillian stepped onto the back rung
of the wheelchair and pushed the
buttons to start the jetpacks. *Vrooom!*

We were off! Jillian was standing
on the back. Stinkball was zooming
along behind us on her board. I had
the front-row seat. *Wheee!*

We sped over speed bumps, popped wheelies past trees, and curled around curves. We went so fast, even the bugs couldn't get out of our way. I sucked at least five or six right up my nose!

"Stinkball!" I shouted. "Open your mouth, and dessert will fly right in!"

Stinkball opened her mouth. Bugs flew in! She gave me a paw thumbs-up.

When we got to the hospital driveway, Jillian slowed to a stop.

"Woohoo!" I jumped out and danced around. "Let's do that again!"

"Get back in the chair," Jillian whispered. "We have to stay quiet."

I sat down, and Jillian pushed me behind a big tree on the side of the hospital. Two windows looked right into the gift shop. From there we could see the shop and also see the front entrance of the hospital.

"Okay, Stinkball," Jillian said. "Just wait by the front door. When Ron and Tanya come, spray them."

"You can do it," I said. "We'll talk you through it."

Stinkball nodded. She hid in the shadow by the front door.

A taxi pulled into the hospital parking lot. A man got out.

Stinkball raised her tail.

"Not this guy, Stinkball!" I said into the headset microphone

She let the guy walk in.

"Nice. You really know how to follow—" I was going to say follow orders. But as soon as I said "follow," Stinkball followed the guy inside.

"No! Come back!" Jillian said.

Stinkball turned around, but the door closed. She was stuck inside.

"Stay right there," Jillian said. "Don't move."

Jillian switched on the mini-screens in front of our goggles. We could see Stinkball's view. She was hiding just inside the front door. A van pulled up.

"Oh, no!" Jillian said. "Look!"

A pest-control van. A big guy carrying a box hopped out of the van.

The guy was going to set out mousetraps! What if Stinkball got caught in a trap? I had to stop him.

I jumped up and whipped off my headset.

"Where are you going?" Jillian said.

I ran up to the guy. "Hey." I started waving my arms. "I just saw a mouse! It was huge. It was this big." I held my arms out. "It had big old nasty teeth. Over here! Follow me!"

The guy followed me around to the back of the hospital.

I made sure he was busy back there. Then I ran back to Jillian.

"Okay, Stinkball," Jillian said into her headset microphone. "New plan. You're going to wait by the door to the gift shop. When Ron and Tanya Crook come in, spray them."

"I'll run and hold the door open for you," I said. "So leave as soon as you spray. This is going to work. Got it?"

Stinkball nodded.

Jillian and I crossed our fingers.

Bear Hugs!

Stinkball was waiting.

We kept one eye on her view through the headset and one eye on the parking lot. As soon as our parents pulled up, we had to be ready to give Stinkball the cue.

Through Stinkball's view, we could see a mom and a little girl get off the elevator and walk toward the gift shop entrance. They didn't even see Stinkball hiding in the shadows by the front door.

"Good, Stinkball. Just stay frozen," Jillian said.

The little girl had a pink cast on her foot.

We could see and hear the whole thing through Stinkball's headset.

"You can pick out anything you want, Carrie!" the mother said. "You've been such a brave girl."

"Oooh," I said. "Get some candy."

Stinkball must have thought I was talking to her. That skunk started walking into the store. She headed toward the candy at the cash register.

"No, Stinkball! Someone will see you."

Stinkball jumped to the side and bumped into a basket of stuffed

92

animals. The basket tipped over, and a teddy bear fell out. The bear was wearing blue jeans, a T-shirt, and sunglasses. He was posed so he was showing off a heart tattoo on his bear bicep.

Stinkball stopped and gasped.

"Go back to the doorway, Stinkball!"

Stinkball couldn't take her eyes off the bear. She waved at him. He didn't wave back.

"Oh, no! I think she likes the bear dude!" I said.

"Stinkball, keep moving!" Jillian said.

We peeked into the gift shop window to get a better view of what was happening.

Stinkball was trying to get the bear's attention. She flexed her muscles. She twirled around. She tried some dance moves.

"We can see you through the window. Stop it," Jillian said into the headset microphone. "Someone will see you."

"He isn't the guy for you, Stinkball," I added. "Trust me! He's going to break your heart."

Stinkball pulled the bear's

sunglasses down and looked deeply into his eyes. There was a little reflection of herself in his eyes. She smiled.

A car pulled up.

It was our parents!

"Go back to the doorway, Stinkball! They're coming!"

Our parents got out and started walking toward the door.

They were going to be there any minute.

"Stinkball, go!" Jillian said.

Stinkball gave the bear a hug. She nuzzled up to him and put her head on his shoulder.

"Mommy, look at that cute stuffed animal!" The little girl in the shop ran over.

"Stinkball, freeze!" I said.

Stinkball froze.

"Aw, she's so cute," the girl said. "I want her."

"The skunk?" the mom asked. "Are you sure?"

"I love her!"

The mom picked Stinkball up by the tail and brought her to the cash register.

Oh, no!

"Ha. I didn't think I had any teddy skunks! That'll be twelve dollars, please." Mr. Packard said. He put Stinkball in a paper shopping bag and tied a ribbon on the handles. He handed the shopping bag to the little girl.

Stinkball had been sold!

Zoom!

Our parents walked into the hospital.

"I'm coming in," I said to
Stinkball. "I repeat: I'm coming in."

"What are you going to do, Billy?"
Jillian asked.

"I have to try something!" I
hopped in the wheelchair and zoomed
into the hospital.

Our parents were right in front
of me. They walked into the gift
shop. They stopped to talk to the

little girl and the mom.

"That's a nice-looking cast," Mom said in a sweet voice. "How did you break your leg?" While she was talking, I saw Dad steal the woman's wallet from her purse. He slipped her wallet into his back pocket. I had to stop them!

"She was a brave girl," the mom said. "She didn't even cry."

I took a left and zoomed into the

bathroom. I grabbed a roll of toilet paper and made a quick disguise.

Time for a ninja move! I zoomed into the gift shop and headed straight for the little girl.

The mom screamed and pulled the girl away. I grabbed the bag out of the girl's hand and tore it open. Stinkball rolled out and landed in a handstand and then jumped into a ninja pose.

Everyone screamed.

Dad and Mom jumped back. "What—?"

Stinkball looked at me. I nodded. She twirled around, lifted her tail, and . . . *Pssssssssssssssssssssssssst!*

She sprayed all over Mom's and Dad's knees and shoes.

Perfect aim! It wasn't the biggest stink, but it was big enough.

"Let's get out of here," Mom said. They both ran out of the store, taking the stink with them.

Mr. Packard, the mom, and the little girl looked at me.

I handed over the mom's wallet. I had picked it from my dad's pocket on the way in. "I believe this is yours," I said.

Stinkball hopped on the back of the wheelchair, and we zoomed out.

Wheeeee!

The Grand Finale

Jillian came running out of the shadows to meet us. She whipped off her headset. "Wow! That was amazing! Great job!"

I bowed. "Couldn't have done it without Stinkball."

Stinkball bowed.

"And you did an awesome job with all your inventions, Jillian." I patted my sister on the back.

Just then a security guard came

walking toward us. He had the pest-control guy with him! The guy had a box of traps.

"Stinkball, hide!"

Stinkball scampered under the wheelchair. Jillian pulled her cap down low to hide her face.

"Hi," the guard said, "We heard there was a skunk around here."

"A skunk?" I looked around. "I might have seen one earlier, but I don't see one now."

Jillian looked around. "Yeah, I don't see any skunks at the moment."

"If you do, let us know," the guard said. "Safety is our biggest concern. We can't have wild animals in the hospital."

"Speaking of safety," Jillian said, "we were just wondering if any babies have ever been stolen from this hospital."

"Babies?" The guard nodded. "About ten years ago, two babies were stolen. Their parents were heartbroken."

Jillian looked at me. I looked at Jillian. Was he talking about us?

"Was it two girls or two boys?"
Jillian asked.

"A boy and a girl," the guard said.
"Twins. Felt terrible about it. Don't
know how those crooks got in to steal
them."

Jillian secretly squeezed my hand.

"Did the police ever find the twins
and bring them back to their real
parents?" I asked.

"I don't think so," the guard said.

My heart was beating fast. I think Jillian's was, too.

"Do you remember the names of the parents?" Jillian asked.

"I do! It was Mr. and Mrs. Deed," the guard said.

"Do you know where they live?" I asked.

The guy thought for a moment. I squeezed my eyes shut, making a wish that he would remember.

"No, I don't," he said. "They might have moved away." He turned to the pest-control man. "I guess the skunk split. We'll call you if we want you to come back."

When they were gone, Jillian whispered, "This is so exciting! Maybe

we were those twins who were stolen.
Maybe our real parents are Mr. and
Mrs. Deed! Maybe they miss us and
have been looking for us for all these
years!"

"How are we going to find them?"
I asked.

"We can do research," she said.
"Come on, let's go back home before
Ron and Tanya get suspicious."

Stinkball came out from under
the wheelchair and looked at us. She
didn't want to be alone.

Just then we heard a noise.

The leaves in the tree above us
rustled.

"Hee-hee-hee."

The squirrel was back.

Stinkball wasn't scared. She

stomped and hissed. She was showing him who was boss.

Then the squirrel made a clicking sound. Ten other squirrels jumped onto the big branch he was standing on. A whole gang of squirrels!

We backed up. The squirrel gang climbed down from the tree. They walked toward poor Stinkball.

The squirrels all had nuts and were tossing them from paw to paw.

"You can do it, Stinkball," Jillian whispered.

"You've got the power," I added.

Stinkball stomped and hissed and arched her back and did a handstand.

The squirrels just laughed. They dug their hind paws into the ground and wound up for the pitch. . . .

Stinkball turned, lifted her tail, and . . . *Psssssssssssssssssssssssssssssssssssssssssssssssssssssst!*

Out came the biggest, baddest stink that ever stank.

The squirrels took off running.

We plugged our noses and cheered.

"Whomp. Whomp. Whomp.
Do it Stinky style.
Whomp. Whomp. Whomp.
Do it Stinky style."

Stinkball, Jillian, and I were
doing the stinky dance when we heard
another noise. . . .

"Don't tell me those bullies are
back," Jillian said.

Two black shapes walked out of
the shadows. Each had a white stripe
down its back.

Stinkball jumped and ran to them.

"Stinkball's mom and dad!" I
exclaimed.

"Her scent must have attracted
them to her," Jillian said. "They must
have been looking for her all this time."

The three skunks sniffed and
nuzzled one another.

My heart was bursting with joy.
We had stopped a robbery. We had
taught a young skunk how to defend

herself. And now that little skunk was back with her parents.

Ah, the joy of doing good deeds!

Little Stinkball was walking away with her parents. She stopped and looked back at us. She smiled.

Their beautiful white stripes were gleaming in the moonlight as they walked out of sight.

"Peace out, dude," I said. "Live long and be stinky."

"Come on, Billy," Jillian said. She hopped onto the back of the wheelchair. "Let's go home. Tomorrow, we can start trying to find Mr. and Mrs. Deed. Then we'll see if they're our real parents."

I stopped. "What if Mr. and Mrs. Deed are our real parents and they gave us away because they didn't like us?"

"Why wouldn't they like us?"

"Maybe you were the Princess of Puke and I was the Prince of Poop," I said.

Jillian gave me a playful punch. "Oh, come on, I'm sure we were very cute babies."

"Okay, then, what if Mr. and Mrs. Deed are our real parents and

they're even worse than Ron and
Tanya Crook? What if they're pirates?
Or zombies? Or creatures from outer
space?"

"Billy, we're nice," Jillian said. "I
bet they're nice, too." She smiled.

"You're right." I nodded. "Who
couldn't love us?"

We did the Stinky-style dance all
the way home.

Secret Extras

SECRET FACTS

Some skunks have spots and swirls instead of stripes.

Male skunks are bigger than females, but females have longer tails.

Baby skunks are called kits or kittens.

SECRET RIDDLE

What do skunks say in church?

Let us spray!

SECRET GAME

Tape the Tail on the Skunky

Make your own Tape the Tail on the Skunky game. You need at least two kids to play.

1. Make a copy of the pictures of the skunk and the tail on pages 118-119, or download the printable page at www. maryamato.com/secret-extras.

2. Have a grown-up help cut out the pictures. Do not cut them out of this book!

3. Put a roll of tape on the back of the skunk and a roll of tape on the back of the tail.

4. Tape the skunk to your friend's back and tell him or her to stand still.

5. Hold on to the tail and stand back-to-back with your friend.
6. Walk twelve steps away from your friend with your eyes closed.
7. After you get to twelve, stop. Keep your eyes closed and turn around, so that you are facing your friend.
8. Walk exactly eleven steps WITH YOUR EYES STILL CLOSED. Do not peek.
9. Keep your eyes closed, and tape the tail gently where you think the skunk's cute little rear end should be. Hopefully, your aim will be good and you will not be taping the tail to your friend's cute little rear end.
10. Okay. Open your eyes.

Did your tail end up in the right place? If so, you get 1,000 points! If it ends up on your friend's arm or leg or cute little rear end, laugh your head off.

STINKY STYLE SONG

Check out the recording of the "Stinky Style" song at www.maryamato.com/secret-extras. Sing along and make sure to add cool dance moves!

Whomp. Whomp. Whomp.
Whomp. Whomp. Whomp.
You're so cool. You're so black.
Got a white stripe down your back.

Whomp. Whomp. Whomp. Do it
   Stinky style.
Whomp. Whomp. Whomp. Do it
   Stinky style.

Stomp your feet. Raise your tail.
You got moves. You will not fail.

Whomp. Whomp. Whomp. Do it
Stinky style.
Whomp. Whomp. Whomp. Do it
Stinky style.

Make a hiss. Stomp your feet.
Arch your back. Jump to the
beat.

Whomp. Whomp. Whomp. Do it
Stinky style.
Whomp. Whomp. Whomp. Do it
Stinky style.
Don't be scared. Don't be blinky.
Turn around and make a
stinky!

Whomp. Whomp. Whomp. Do it
Stinky style.

Whomp. Whomp. Whomp. Do it
   Stinky style.

Whomp. Whomp. Whomp.
   Oh, yeah.